the misadventures of
CHICO CHUGG

by
janet roberts

scribbles by
ed naujokas

Janet Roberts is a mother of three children and an ex primary school deputy head. She retired early, sold her house and now lives on a narrowboat with her husband Mike and Chico their Jack Russell.

BARKING BOOKS UK

The Misadventures of Chico Chugg
SECOND PAPERBACK EDITION

A CIP catalogue record for this title is available from the British Library.

ISBN: 978-0-9574594-0-3

First Published in 2011 by
Olympia Publishers

This edition published by
BARKING BOOKS UK
PO Box 6218
Coventry
CV3 9HX

2012

Printed in Great Britain
by XPD Print Limited
www.xpdprint.co.uk

Dedication

In memory of a dog called Chico Bulefante.

To James

love

Jan + Chico x

Acknowledgements

I would like to thank Hanslope Primary School, St Nicholas Primary School and Dunchurch Junior School for reading 'The Misadventures of Chico Chugg' to their children. It was their positive responses that gave me the confidence to approach publishers with this book.

Thanks also to my three children. Sarah and James who encouraged me all the way and Edward for his beautiful illustrations. Thanks to my dad, the best storyteller I ever heard, he has always been my inspiration. Finally, thanks to my husband Mike without whose continuing love, support and patience I would have never have had the opportunity to write and live our wonderful life with Chico aboard our narrowboat 'Wah Wah Chugg'.

Introduction.

My Dad was the best storyteller I ever heard. With a few simple words he could make my childhood toys come alive involving them in amazing and believable adventures. I have always tried to instill that same love of stories he gave to me in my own children and the many hundreds of children I have taught over the years.

One of my favourite things is reading aloud, seeing children's faces light up as they use their imagination to form the words into pictures in their heads.

Now after years of reading many books by inspiring authors I've finally had the time to write my own.

Chico is the name of my own pet dog. The stories are told through his eyes, looking at life with the innocence of a small dog and engaging his audience by addressing them directly. The stories are as enjoyable to read aloud as they are to read to yourself, so children from five years upwards can enjoy the funny situations that Chico often finds himself in.

I sincerely hope you enjoy reading my books as much as I have enjoyed writing them and I wish everyone could have a little 'Chico' in their lives!

There are six books in the series:

The Misadventures of Chico Chugg.
Chico Chugg the Hero.
Chico Chugg and the Visitors.
Chico Chugg goes to Yelvertoft.
Chico Chugg goes to Cropredy.
Chico Chugg learns French.

CONTENTS

CHAPTER ONE
the chugg family

Hello! My name is Chico. I'm a small dog, mostly white with a few brown spots. I live with a family called 'the Chuggs'. The Chuggs are no ordinary family, they live an exciting life together, having fun and adventures every day but it wasn't always like this. I remember the day I first met them.

I'd been in a pet shop for almost a week and was really missing my brothers and sisters. They'd been sold within the first couple of days but I was still there. I just couldn't understand it. When people came into the shop I'd jump about excitedly barking at them so they'd notice me and see how lovely I was. I'd wag my tail madly hoping they'd choose me, but they *always* chose my brothers and sisters who sat there quietly. Perhaps I was doing it wrong? Maybe I needed to be calmer, so I decided the next time people came into the shop, I'd sit quietly and see what happened.

It was early one morning, I was just settling down for a nap after breakfast when a family came in chatting and laughing. It consisted of a boy and a girl who looked very alike. They had the same shaped face and features. Their eyes smiled in the same way as they talked excitedly about all the pets in the shop. Their Mum and Dad looked friendly, and I liked the way they leaned their heads together as they spoke to each other.

From the little 'oohs' and 'aahs' as the children looked at

the hamsters it was apparent that they were going to buy one. I was feeling very lonely and wishing they would buy me instead. I decided I needed to grab their attention, so in spite of my previous decision to sit quietly, I started to bark and jump around…

As I did so I knocked over my water bowl, which caught the edge of my food bowl making it flip over and land on my tail. Ouch! It really hurt! I let out a loud howl and ran round and round trying to lick the end of my tail where the pain was coming from. With all this noise the little girl spotted me.

"Oh Mummy," she said. "Look! Doesn't this little puppy look cute? Look how he's running round and round. Isn't he funny?"

As she came up to me I realised that now I'd got their attention I'd better be on my best behaviour so I stopped chasing around, went up to her and wagged my tail. I started to lick her hand as she went to stroke me.

"Ah! That tickles! Look Mummy isn't he cute? Can we buy this puppy instead of a hamster?"

"Now hang on a minute!" said the dad. "We agreed you could both have a pet, but a dog? That's far more responsibility than a hamster! You'd have to take him for walks and play with him every day, and what about holidays? We'd have to go places where we could take the dog as well or put him in kennels. And I saw what he was doing just then, he's a bit excitable isn't he? If we got a dog wouldn't it be sensible to get one that's a bit calmer?" I could see he was looking concerned.

"Oh, but we would look after him properly!" chorused the children. "He's calmer now and he's *so* cute! Look… he likes us!"

I was trying very hard to sit still and wagging my tail as fast as I could, forgetting all about how much it hurt. This looked like it would be a lovely family to live with and I was really hoping they would buy me. The Mum had joined the children and was stroking me while I wagged my tail and licked her hand.

"Oh, Harry, look at him! He really is cute isn't he?" she remarked. "He may be a bit lively, but he's got character and he'd be such good company for me and the children when you're working late." Dad looked at me and could see he was fighting a losing battle, even Mum had fallen for me, so I looked up at him jumping and wagging my tail to show that I liked him too.

"What would we call him?" asked Mum.

"Oh, I know," shouted the boy, "what about 'Chico' after the dog Dad had when he was little." I guess he was thinking this might help persuade Dad to buy me.

"Chico was a Jack Russell dog, too, wasn't he Dad? You always said what fun you had with him when you were little..." Dad looked more closely at me.

"Come to think of it, he even looks a bit like my old Chico." He said with a smile.

"Chico it is then!" said Mum. "I think it really suits him."

Yes 'Chico' ... I liked it as well. Now I'd got a name I was already beginning to feel part of the family. Dad finally gave in.

"Oh, Okay. I suppose we could give him a try, but he can't be allowed to get into mischief! If *you* don't look after him properly..." Dad said looking at the two children, "he will be coming straight back to the pet shop!"

After Dad had paid and the children had chosen a basket and lead, Dad carried me out of the shop towards the car. I licked his ear and snuggled into his neck.

"Hmm," said Dad in a serious voice. "I hope we've done the right thing." But I noticed a slight smile on his face as he tickled me behind my ears and that was when I knew that Dad and I would be great friends.

On the way home in the car everyone chatted away happily and I soon discovered the family were called the 'Chuggs' and that it was the children's birthday and I was their present. They were twins and that was why they looked so alike, I was later to discover that the girl was twenty minutes older than the boy and, because of this, felt she was the boss and often liked to tell him what to do. Their names were Charlotte and Jimmy and it was their fifth birthday. They had been asking for a pet for a long time, but with Mum working full time as a teacher and Dad teaching music and playing in bands, it meant that whatever pet they got would be their total responsibility, that was why a hamster had seemed such a good idea.

"Hamsters don't need too much attention." Dad had said.

harry

Now they had chosen me I was determined to prove that I would be easy to look after and much more fun than a hamster. I really wanted to stay with this family and definitely didn't want to go back to the pet shop!

Unfortunately the journey home was a little more eventful than anyone could have predicted.

I sat in the back of the car between Jimmy and Charlotte. They laughed and giggled as they stroked and fussed me. I was having a wonderful time and really enjoying all the attention. I was so excited that I had a family at last! Mum told them not to let me lick their faces as it was 'unhygienic', but they ignored her and encouraged me by rubbing their faces next to mine.

Jimmy was as lively as I was, he was jumping about tickling me, and I started to bark with excitement.

"Be careful, Jimmy!" shouted Charlotte. "You are getting Chico too excited now and mind he doesn't get tangled up in your seatbelt!"

"Oh, he loves it!" Jimmy shouted back as he continued to tickle me.

As I got more and more excited I started to notice that we were moving quite fast. I hadn't been in a car before and I wasn't sure if I liked it. I was starting to feel a bit dizzy and my tummy was starting to feel strange. The more I jumped about the more uncomfortable my tummy felt. I decided that perhaps I needed to sit quietly and then maybe this strange feeling would go away, but I was enjoying all the attention from Jimmy, so the more he tickled and hugged me the more I jumped. This is when it all went wrong!

Just when Charlotte started to get really cross, the strange feeling in my tummy seemed to erupt...

"Eeeuuurgh!" groaned Jimmy.

It suddenly went very quiet in the car and I looked up to see everyone staring at me with shocked expressions on their faces.

"Quick, Harry, pull over!" shouted Mum. "Chico's been sick all over Jimmy!"

"Told you, you were making him too excited." Whined Charlotte.

"Oh shut up!" replied Jimmy. "I was only having fun."

"Yes but look what happened!" The twins started to argue.

"Quiet both of you!" shouted Mum, "Let's get this mess cleared up."

When Dad had pulled the car over I was starting to feel better, but everyone else was frowning and looking a little pale.

Mum cleared up the mess as best she could and we all drove on in silence. I kept looking at Jimmy who was now looking out of the window ignoring me. I somehow felt as if I was in disgrace and decided I definitely didn't like cars and would try to avoid being in one ever again.

When we got to their house they put my basket in the kitchen and I thought that maybe it was a good idea to lie down quietly. The children seemed disappointed as they tried to encourage me to jump about again.

"Now just leave him alone!" warned Mum. "He's had quite enough excitement for one day. Let him get used to his new home, this must be very strange and new for him, remember."

So the children left me alone and I watched them as they went about their day.

Later on, Charlotte and Jimmy both came to say goodnight to me before they went to bed and, after watching them both trudge upstairs,

I snuggled down feeling quite exhausted after my exciting day. Suddenly I noticed someone else standing over me.

"How're you doing there, little fella?"

It was Dad. He bent down and started stroking me gently on the head.

"We're going to have some real adventures aren't we, Chico?" he said. "You sleep well. I think you're going to like it in your new home!"

And you know what? I think he was right.

After a while, everyone seemed to have forgotten about the incident in the car. I soon discovered that life with the Chuggs was fun. The twins played with me as soon as they came home from school and always took me for a walk after tea. Mum, whose name was Hilary, was a primary school teacher and Dad, Harry, was a music teacher and played in local bands. They were both out all day and the children were at school so I was on my own a great deal. Mum did try, most days, to pop home for ten minutes at lunchtime so I could go out in the garden. Weekends were great. We all went for long walks and I sat on the children's laps while they played computer games and watched TV.

The months went by happily until the next summer when Mum announced she wanted to go on holiday to Spain. The children were disappointed when she said they couldn't take me with them.

"Oh Mum! We can't go on holiday without Chico," they moaned. "He'd hate living in kennels and we'd miss him *so* much!" So it was agreed that we would stay in England. The next night Dad and the twins were sitting around the kitchen table looking at holiday brochures and Mum was checking the internet on her laptop. After looking at some seaside hotels Jimmy and Charlotte were concerned.

"The beach would be fun for us because we could make sandcastles and stuff, but I bet Chico'll get bored, especially if you and Mum just sunbathe all day!" grumbled Jimmy. It went quiet, everyone was thinking hard. Suddenly, Dad snapped his fingers.

"I know," he said. "What about a canal holiday? There would be lots for everyone to do and even Chico could join in with that. You could start that book you've always wanted to write Hilary, what do you think?"

"Ooh, it'll be like that holiday we had when we were first married," replied an enthusiastic Mum. "Yes it was great fun. You two are going to love it!" she said, grinning at the twins.

I had no idea what a canal holiday was, but I soon found out.

A few weeks later, off we went for our week's holiday. We didn't have to drive too far before Dad turned off down a narrow driveway between some trees. At the end of the driveway the road widened out into a small car park and that was when I saw what Mum had meant by a 'canal holiday'. Running along the side of the car park was what looked like a narrow river with brightly coloured boats tied up along it's edge. Jimmy and Charlie were very excited as a man showed us to a boat. Oh this did look like it would be fun.

The twins enjoyed helping Dad with the boat, learning to steer by pushing the brightly painted tiller from side to side and using a long hose to fill up the water tank. They pulled the boat to the bank with ropes when we stopped for the day and hammered big metal pins into the bank to tie the boat to overnight. They discovered they had a love of fishing when Dad let them have a go at it one day. Charlotte always seemed to catch the biggest fish, much to Jimmy's annoyance.

"You're a natural!" said Dad smiling, while Jimmy looked on with a cross face.

Mum started to write her book and tapped away intently on her laptop as we chugged peacefully along. By the end of the holiday she had managed to write the first chapter of a storybook for children. Dad loved having time to write lyrics for some songs he was composing and I loved snoozing on the back deck with everyone around me, feeling the boat's engine rumbling through my tummy. It was over all too soon.

A few months after our holiday, things started to change at home. It happened so gradually I didn't even notice it to begin with... First Mum stopped popping home at lunchtime to see me, so I was on my own *all* day. Dad had to put a special flap in the door to the garden, so I could go out when I needed to. Mum also seemed to be working every night, 'doing school work' as she put it. She never had time to work on her book anymore. The children would go into their rooms playing on their computers or go to their friends' houses to play. Dad seemed to be out most nights playing with his bands or helping youngsters practise with their bands. I didn't get taken out for walks so often now and spent a lot of time alone in my basket.

I often tried to get everyone's attention by barking or jumping on their laps but they would say "Not *now*, Chico!" Even weekends weren't so much fun. Mum started to work even more on her laptop, Dad was tired during the day because he was getting in late most nights and the twins went out to their friends to play because they said it was boring at home. I was beginning to feel very neglected and the atmosphere in the house had changed from happy and bubbly to dreary and dull. That is until one day when Mum came home from school even more exhausted than usual.

Her class had completely worn her out and she'd stayed late at school working. She didn't have to pick the children up from after school club on Tuesdays because they came

19

home with Marc and his mum. Marc lived next door to Jimmy and Charlotte and was Jimmy's best friend.

Mum got home and was fed up to find that Dad had already left to play in one of his bands.

The children were due home in five minutes and there was no tea ready!

She found a small pizza in the back of the almost empty freezer and sat down to have a cup of tea while it cooked. Just as she was beginning to relax, Jimmy and Charlotte burst into the house. I jumped up to greet them and they stroked my head, said a quick 'Hi' and then rushed off into the kitchen.

"Is tea ready Mum?" shouted Jimmy.

"Almost," replied Mum as she got up to check the pizza.

"Not pizza *again!*" whined Charlotte.

"'Fraid so," said Mum. "If Dad had gone shopping today you could have had burgers."

"Oh burgers would have been much nicer," continued Charlotte. "I'm fed up with pizza, that's all we ever seem to eat."

"Don't moan," whispered Jimmy. "Can't you see how tired Mum looks? Its fine Mum don't worry pizza's *my* favourite," he said out loud.

"Well it's alright for you then isn't it!" hissed Charlotte. I could see where this was going, another argument between the twins!

Normally Mum would have told them to stop arguing by now, but she seemed quite distracted. The twins seemed to notice that she wasn't paying attention so stopped arguing and sat down to eat. Charlotte started to tell Mum about her day, but she didn't seem to be listening. Jimmy tried next to tell Mum that he was going to play at Marc's house after tea, but again she didn't seem to hear him. By the time they were finishing their pizza she was already typing on her laptop.

"Mum, you're not listening!" moaned Charlotte. "Jimmy's just said he's going to Marc's house after tea, but you always say we have to do our reading practice before we can go and play,"

"Oh thanks Charlotte!" said Jimmy crossly. "Mum, I'll do my reading later I promise, please let me go, I won't be too long, Oh please Mum, *please*!"

I could see Mum had a really fed up look on her face. She looked like that quite often these days.

"Fine!' she shouted. "I'm *too* tired to argue and I've got all this work to do for school tomorrow. Jimmy, you can go but make sure you're back in one hour and then do your reading as soon as you get in."

"See you later," shouted Jimmy. He stuck his tongue out at Charlotte and the front door banged as he rushed out.

"I'm going to my room!" replied a sulky Charlotte and stomped off upstairs.

I went and sat in my basket, it was clear no one was going to take me for a walk!

As the kitchen went quiet Mum leaned back in her chair and rubbed her eyes,

"Oh Chico, this is ridiculous," she said. "I'm always tired, always working, never have time for the twins and I can't remember the last time I sat down with their dad."

Suddenly she banged the table with her hand and shouted,

"IT'S TIME FOR ACTION!"

I jumped out of my basket and started to bark and run around in circles. Mum had a smile on her face for the first time in ages and I had a feeling that maybe things were about to change around here. I was hoping it would be for the better!

CHAPTER TWO

mum's idea

When Dad got home later that night Mum was up and waiting for him. I was sitting on her lap and we were watching telly.

"You're still up!" said Dad. I knew he was surprised to see that Mum hadn't gone to bed already.

"Are you happy?" was Mum's immediate reply. Taken aback, Dad looked like he wasn't sure what she meant.

"Happy with what?" he replied.

"Your life, work, home, you know… the time you have for yourself… everything!"

"Where's all this coming from?" asked Dad, starting to look a bit worried.

Mum told him what had happened when she'd got home from work and how it had made her feel that something had to be done to bring the family back together again. I was listening intently.

"When was the last time you really felt we were having fun as a family?" she asked.

Dad frowned, concentrating.

"Last year on that narrowboat, I expect," he replied.

"I agree!" Replied Mum excitedly.

"So this is what I propose – we buy a boat of our own!"

"You mean so we can go on the canals whenever we want?"

"No, not just for holidays," answered Mum. "I mean *live* on a boat!"

Now Dad was looking really confused, his eyebrows danced up and down. I couldn't believe what I was hearing! I could imagine us all staying on a boat for the long school holidays, but did Mum mean permanently? Dad was looking unsure and I must say I was wondering what she would say next.

"We could sell the house, give up work, home tutor the children and have more time together again," said a very excited Mum. So she *did* mean permanently.

"Don't worry," she said. "I've got a plan!" She showed him a piece of paper covered in writing. This is what it said:

- give up work
- sell the house
- home tutor the children
- spend less money because a boat is cheap to run
- have savings in the bank from selling the house
- hilary finish writing book
- harry write more songs
- read whenever we want to
- start hobbies again- draw, paint, sew, fish
- travel whenever we want to
- have friends to stay for holidays
- have adventures

At the bottom of the page in capital letters was written:

HAVE MORE TIME TOGETHER
AS A FAMILY!!!

There was a stony silence as he finished reading the list. Mum was looking at Dad and me with a worried expression on her face.

What do you think Dad's reaction was?

His serious face slowly grew a smile, then a grin and then he made me jump with a big belly laugh!

"Ha ha! It's brilliant!" he shouted. "A little short on detail but...it's brilliant!"

I started to bark and chase my tail, Mum started to laugh as well and they both swayed from side to side as they hugged each other. There was such a commotion that for a minute we didn't notice Charlotte and Jimmy standing in the doorway.

"What's all the noise about?" complained a sleepy-eyed Charlotte.

"Something momentous has happened," beamed Dad. "Remember how much fun we used to have when we first got Chico? Going for walks, playing games together and having fun, well it's not been like that lately has it? Mum's always working and so am I. We hardly see each other any more. I'm worried that you two are growing up so quickly and Mum and I are missing it. Mum and I both feel we need to be together more as a family." The twins looked at each other confused. "Well, Mum's had a genius idea!"

"We're not moving house are we?" asked Charlotte.

"Well sort of..." replied Mum. "One way we can all be together more is if me and Dad give up work and there is a way we can do this... If we sell the house."

"But where would we live?" asked Charlotte, frowning.

"Well," Mum continued, "we'd use the money from selling the house to buy a narrowboat and there'd be enough left over to have some savings in the bank." She paused again, looking at the twins carefully, and then went on. "We could live off our savings and any money Dad makes from his gigs and songs. I also want to finish my book and try and sell some copies, so that may bring in some money and I could always do odd days of supply teaching. You know, fill in for teachers who are sick." Jimmy and Charlotte just stared. I couldn't tell if they liked the idea or not.

"What about school?" asked Jimmy.

"Well I've thought about that. Dad and I could teach you at home so you wouldn't have to go to school. Think of all the adventures we could have!" Jimmy couldn't contain himself,

"What? No school?" he yelled. "What a great idea! When could we do it? Have you found a boat yet? Wait till I tell Marc!"

"Hang on a minute Jimmy, I'm glad you're so enthusiastic but there's still lots to discuss and organise," said Mum, but Jimmy didn't hear her, he'd already danced away into the lounge shouting, "Yippee! No school!" Charlotte hadn't said anything and she didn't look excited or enthusiastic.

"What's wrong, Charlotte?" said Mum. "You loved it on the boat last summer."

"But that was a holiday," Charlotte said quietly. "It'd be different if we *lived* on a boat... what about our friends, when would we see them? There's not much room on a boat so where would we put all our stuff? And I *love* school, I can't imagine never going again... It's alright for Jimmy, he doesn't like it anyway, but I love it!"

Poor Charlotte! I tried to cheer her up by licking her toes as they stuck out from underneath her pyjamas but I don't think she even noticed. Mum came over and gave her a hug, "Listen sweetie," she said gently. "I know you'd miss school and your friends at first, but honestly, Dad and I could make learning just as much fun as it is at school and your friends could come and visit us whenever you want them to. The main thing is that we would be together more as a family."

Charlotte didn't look convinced and looked like she was going to cry. In the silence we could hear Jimmy, upstairs now, still jumping about and shouting, "Yippee no school!"

"Alright," said Dad. "Lets leave this until tomorrow. It's too late at night to talk now, lets sleep on it and see how we feel in the morning."

So everyone went up to bed leaving me downstairs to curl up in my basket wondering what would happen next.

The next morning was Saturday and Mum and Dad got up exceptionally early, It didn't look as though they had slept much as they still looked tired. I was excited because it meant an early breakfast and walk with Dad and, by the time we got back, the twins had only just got up.

This turned out to be a very unusual Saturday. Instead of the twins rushing off to ballet and football, Mum going shopping and Dad going for a sound check for his gig later that night, we all got in the car together with Mum announcing that we were going to look at narrowboats, to get a clearer idea of what it would be like to live on one all the time.

"The boat we went on last year was very basic," said Mum.
"I just want us to go and look at the sort of boat we could afford to buy if we sold the house.

It would be bigger and much more comfortable." she said brightly, trying to convince Charlotte.

It was very quiet in the car, no one was speaking and I was beginning to get worried wondering how things would turn out. I always sat quietly in the back of the car now. I had never forgotten what had happened on the drive home from the pet shop. The marina was in a village called Crick and wasn't far from where we lived. When we got there the sun was shining and Charlotte was starting to look slightly more relaxed.

There was a very friendly lady called Michele in the sales office who had a black spaniel dog. While she showed everyone pictures and details of some boats, the little black spaniel started to talk to me.

"Bonjour, my name is Henri," he said, pronouncing his name 'Onree'. "What's yours?"

"Oh, I'm Chico, Chico Chugg," I replied.

"I am living 'ere on a boat. And you?"

I could just make out what he was saying, but he spoke in a way I had never heard before. Just as I was about to answer the twins rushed up and started patting Henri.

"Oh aren't you beautiful!" exclaimed Charlotte. "What's your name then?"

"His names Henri," said Michele. "We bought him when we lived in France and he came back to England with us a few years ago." *Now* I understood why Henri sounded so strange, he was from France!

"Well, I'm not sure if we are going to live on a boat yet," I told him. "It all depends if we can find a nice one. Do you like living on a boat, Henri?"

"Ah oui," replied Henri. "It's much better zan living in an 'ouse. Always zere is someone close by!"

Hmm yes, that sounded very appealing.

henri

Dad had told us we would be looking at older boats that weren't so expensive. He'd often say, with a cheeky grin on his face that he felt he was quite a 'handy man.'

"I could do any work the boat needs by myself!" he said confidently.

"I could help too!" said an enthusiastic Jimmy who was still very excited about Mum's idea.

"You could teach me how to use a saw and I could help build stuff."

"I don't think it'll be that easy!" snapped Charlotte.

Anyway you'd have to be careful, Jimmy, you know how clumsy you are!

Working with hammers and saws can be very dangerous. If we're out somewhere on the boat we won't be able to drive you to hospital if you cut your thumb off you know!"

"Oh Charlotte!" said Mum. "No one's going to hospital. Let's just wait and see what the boats are like, maybe Dad won't have to do too much work on it anyway." Mum hoped so, she knew exactly who Jimmy got his accident-prone tendencies from.

Michele said we could go and look at the boats now if we wanted to, so we followed her down to the marina where dozens of prettily painted narrow boats were lined up neatly at their moorings.

It didn't start well. The first boat we looked at was lovely on the outside, painted in traditional boat colours of blue, red and green, but inside it was a different story.

It was dark and dingy because of the small circular windows called portholes. There was a fusty smell and the carpets and curtains were old and faded. The bathroom was small and the tiles looked stained. The kitchen had battered cupboards and looked like it would need a lot doing to it to get it looking nice.

"I could probably do *some* of the work," said Dad, looking concerned.

I couldn't imagine us living on it at all, maybe on a holiday for a few weeks, but not all the time as our home. I could tell Charlotte hated it by the look on her face! Even Jimmy didn't look so keen.

Mum was very disappointed. The next boat was even worse, it didn't even look that nice on the outside with the paint chipped off and rust appearing in lots of places. Oh dear, now Charlotte looked like she had completely lost interest and even Mum was beginning to look a bit disheartened.

"Perhaps we could afford to spend a bit more?" said Dad. "Get a newer boat that doesn't need so much work doing on it. What about that one over there?" Dad pointed towards a boat moored by itself with a 'For Sale' sign in the window. It was just one colour, a pale blue, with nice big rectangular windows and lovely pots of flowers on the roof. Its name was painted on the side in simple letters and it was called 'Whichwey'.

"Well actually you're in luck," said Michele. "It only went on sale today. It is more expensive, but if you want to look around it I'm sure the owners wouldn't mind."

So suddenly we were climbing down into a light and welcoming boat. All the walls were covered in a pale modern wood and the large windows let in lots of sunshine. The doors of the kitchen cupboards were a shiny red and it was clean and fresh. The bathroom was the same size as ours at home. It even had a full sized shower finished with bright white tiles. The two bedrooms were small, but pretty.

The first one had a door that, when opened, revealed a space the exact length of a single bed with just enough space to walk down the side. There was another single bed above it. Opposite the small bedroom was an area where a small desk had been built in.

"We could put our computers here and make a little studio," suggested Dad. "I could write my songs and Mum could write her book."

The next bedroom was the exact size of a small double bed, which was built in right up against the wall with enough room to walk down the other side. At the end of the bed was a small set of drawers on one side and a small dressing table on the other. In the middle were two little steps up to two glass doors that opened out onto the front deck.

The curtains were new and light and it had a lovely fresh smell of wood. There was a lounge with a black stove in the corner that had a fire glowing in it.

"How long is the boat?' Dad asked the owners.

"Just over twenty-one metres," they told us.

"Is that about the same length as a bus?" asked Jimmy. I could see he was trying to visualize just how long the boat was.

"Actually almost two buses," replied Dad.

"I'd forgotten how narrow these boats are!" said Charlotte quietly with a frown of disapproval on her face. "I bet Dad could only just lie down across the width of the boat!"

"Oh Charlotte," said Dad, "that's why they're called *narrow*boats. At least we've got a bit more headroom on this boat than the last two. Look my head's not touching the ceiling at all!"

The back deck was large enough for more than two people to stand on and Michele said that it was called a cruiser stern. I decided it would be a great place for me to sit when we were chugging.

"What do you think of this boat Charlotte?" asked Mum.

"Oh, it's OK," replied Charlotte. "It's certainly nicer than the other two, but it's so much smaller than our house!"

The owners of the boat were very friendly and everyone looked like they were starting to relax at last. We discovered that the boat was four years old and that the people had had it made especially for them when they retired. However recently the lady had developed painful knees and was finding it more and more difficult to get on and off, so that's why they had decided to sell it.

While they were chatting I was beginning to get bored so I decided to go back outside and see if I could find Henri.

I pulled gently against my lead and it began to extend. I knew it would it let me go quite a long way before Dad noticed.

As I got up the steps onto the back deck I noticed that the boat next door had its back doors open too. I could just hear the gentle thud, thud, thud of its engine. It was a very pretty boat with beautiful paintings on the inside of its back doors. The paintings were of castles on hillsides surrounded by rivers. I couldn't quite see inside the boat but I could smell something that made my mouth water. Could it be? Yes it was… bacon! My favourite. I began to feel really hungry. Before I knew it I found myself climbing carefully down into the other boat.

What I hadn't realised was that, as I'd crossed onto the other boat, my lead had wrapped around a handle. This was the handle that you pushed to make the engine go faster. As I walked down the steps towards the delicious smell the lead was pulling the handle down and the engine was starting to rev up.

This is when it all became a bit of a blur…

As I jumped down the last step, the lever was tugged down almost as far as it could go and the engine roared!

I panicked, tried to scramble backwards up the stairs, got caught up in the lead and pulled it even tighter, the engine roared louder still. It scared me so much that I started to bark and chased madly round getting more and more tangled as I did so.

Suddenly a man's bald head appeared through a little door on the side of the boat and he didn't look very happy.

"WHAT'S GOING ON?" he bellowed. By now the twins and Mum and Dad had appeared. I was still barking, but had stopped jumping about because my lead was so caught up I couldn't move.

"Oh, Chico, what are you doing?" shouted Jimmy as he ran to me. "Shhhh now you silly dog, you're all caught up!" I can tell you I was shaking long after Mum and Dad had apologised and calmed down the owner of the boat.

"It's alright," he said at last, "no harm done."

The man said his name was Stan and that he had lived alone on his boat since his wife died. He even invited us all to go inside and look around it. Mum carried me in her arms as she walked around the boat and I noticed Stan was keeping a wary eye on me. The children thought the boat was beautiful. Although it was very old, it had been lovingly cared for. There were plates on the walls that had colourful, silk ribbons threaded around the edges of them. Very shiny brass kettles and ornaments were placed around the black stove and delicate lace framed every window.

Dad fell in love with the intricate and shiny engine 'oohing' and 'aahing' as Stan explained how it worked.

After looking at Stan's boat we went and found Michele again in the sales office.

"Well, did you like "Whichwey?" she asked.

"She's perfect!" replied Mum.

"There's just one more vital question," said Dad. "Have you got any residential moorings here? We'll want to travel around the canals for the summer but we'll need to moor somewhere over the winter months. I guess it's impossible to move around if the canal freezes."

"A residential mooring *has* just become available for you to use in a couple of months," answered Michele.

"Well that settles it!" said an excited Dad. "Perfect! This feels like it's meant to be, a lovely boat and a mooring and not too far from all our family and friends. We can keep the car here and get about as normal when we are moored!"

It was very different in the car on our way home. Instead of a stony silence there was chatter between Mum and Dad about how and where they could put things. Charlotte was still quiet and Jimmy was stroking and talking to me while I looked at him excitedly.

"Well Chico, what do you think then? Do you think you'd like living on a boat? You wouldn't be on your own so much would you? I bet you'd like, that wouldn't you?"

As a reply I wagged my tail and licked Jimmy's hand.

"See Charlotte, even Chico wants to go and live on a boat," said Jimmy.

"Ok Jimmy, leave your sister alone now, she'll come round to it eventually," said Mum. I hopped so, but I had a feeling it may take her a while.

The atmosphere became more and more intense over the next few weeks as Mum and Dad got excited about the boat idea. They had discussions with the twins some evenings about how they thought their lives might change. Charlotte didn't always agree but gradually she started to soften towards the idea. This first happened one Saturday afternoon when her best friend, Emily, came round to play. I heard Charlotte tell Emily what we were planning to do. Charlotte was surprised by Emily's reaction, instead of Emily agreeing with Charlottes attitude she said that she wished her mum and dad would do something so exciting. She saw very little of her mum and dad as they were always working and she was often at the child minders.

"How exciting to learn stuff at home from your mum and dad. Think of all the adventures you will have living on a boat." She had said enviously.

Time passed quickly and before long the house went up for sale.

Mum and Dad handed in their notices at work and everyone had to sort through their belongings and decide what they would keep. Space is limited on a boat and they couldn't possibly keep everything. Imagine having to get rid of *all* your furniture and most of your books and toys!

The last school day of the summer term arrived and Charlotte said sad goodbyes to her friends.

"Don't worry, sweetie!" Mum said when she got home from school that day. "Your friends can always come and see us."

"Yes, but will they *want* to?" murmured Charlotte.

The house sale went through quickly and we were moving onto the boat on the second Monday of the summer holidays. Mum and Dad had sold most of the furniture and given away lots of their things to friends and to charity shops. It had been hard for the twins, but they had started to realise that actually when they were forced to decide what to keep it hadn't been so difficult after all. They had to admit they hadn't played with lots of their toys for a long time and they only needed to keep a few.

Finally, moving day arrived and I was very excited, as were Mum, Dad and Jimmy. Charlotte still wasn't happy. We waved goodbye to our old house and set off for new adventures onboard 'Whichwey'.

It took a couple of days for us to unpack all our things. Whichwey seemed to have lots of cleverly concealed storage spaces and the twins enjoyed seeing who could find the next hidden cupboard. Jimmy found that his bottom bunk hinged up to reveal a large storage space under his bed, Charlotte found a hidden drawer under the dining room bench seat and Mum loved the way the table and bench seats made into an extra double bed.

"We could use this when people come to stay!" she said. Dad said he was surprised at how much storage space there was and how all their belongings seemed to fit so well. The only thing that I found strange was the feeling you had as the boat rocked from side to side when people moved about. I remembered I hadn't liked it on our holiday, but hopefully I would get used to it, it didn't appear to be worrying Charlotte and Jimmy. They put my basket by the stove in the lounge, so I would be nice and warm and I was very happy. Even Charlotte seemed a little happier.

We spent the next few days settling in. Dad had said we should stay moored at Crick, before we set off on a holiday, to get used to how everything worked in the boat.

"It will be much better if we iron out any problems while we are moored here," he said. "At least we have the car, so if we need to go and buy anything we can still get to the shops."

Through all the hustle and bustle we began to learn how to move around the boat without getting in each other's way or bumping ourselves on cupboards and shelves. The twins soon discovered that things needed to be put away if they weren't being used otherwise the boat became untidy very quickly. Mum said that on a boat it's called 'stowing away' which somehow made it more fun than 'tidying up'. It also took a few nights to get used to all the strange groaning and creaking sounds Whichwey made, as she cooled down in the evening and warmed up again in the morning.

"It's like she's talking to us!" Jimmy observed and he was right, that was just what it sounded like!

The water that came out of the taps in the kitchen and bathroom came from a water tank that was hidden away under the front deck. We discovered that we had to fill it up every three days.

"I don't have to have a shower every day," Jimmy told Mum helpfully. "The water would last longer if I had one a week."

"Nice try young man!" Mum had replied. "But I think we'd all rather you had a shower every day."

The toilet was different from the one at home. It had a button to flush it and a sort of box underneath it that came out. The responsibility for emptying it had fallen to Dad.

"I will do anything but that!" Mum had stated on the first day.

Dad had bought a satellite dish for the television, installed it on the roof of the boat and with a little help from the twins tuned it in.

"A little more to the left...no, right...stop!" they had yelled out of the hatch door when he had tried to align it. It was worth it, though, we had a great picture and more channels than we'd had at home!

I noticed that Charlotte's mood improved a bit as the days went by and Whichwey began to feel more like home. She seemed to enjoy seeing more of Mum and Dad and was even getting on better with Jimmy.

One afternoon as Charlotte, Mum and me were out for a walk around the marina Mum said, "You seem a bit happier, sweetie, do you think you're going to like our new life?"

Charlotte thought for a minute and said, "It's better than I thought it would be, I think it'll be alright".

"Well," replied Mum, giving Charlotte's hand a squeeze, "that's good enough for now."

So this was it, the start of our new life. I was excited and couldn't wait to see how different it might be from our old one. Would we be happy all living so closely together? Would we have more fun? What sorts of adventures would we have? Only time would tell.

CHAPTER THREE

gran saves the day

Dad had bought lots of different maps of canals and on the Monday morning a week after we'd moved aboard we all sat around the table to plan our first journey. As Dad was explaining how to read a map and work out distances, Mum's mobile phone rang. It was Gran and she was asking how we were settling in.

planning our journey

Now, I haven't told you about Gran yet have I? She is Mum's mum. Her name is Dotty and she used to come to our house every Sunday for dinner. Dad would pick her up from her old people's home, which was not far away, and she would stop all afternoon insisting on being taken back in time for tea. Dad seemed to be the only person in the family she liked and she was always sweet to him, smiling and laughing at his silly jokes, whilst with everyone else, even Mum, she was grumpy and always seemed to be cross about something.

I remember the first time I met Gran… it was a disaster! I had only been with the Chuggs for a couple of days and was still very excited about my new home.

Now, Gran walks with the aid of a walking stick and as she came into the kitchen on her Sunday visit I ran out of my basket jumping and barking, pleased to see a new visitor.
She tried to move quickly to avoid standing on me and caught her foot on her walking stick.

This is when it all became a bit of a blur…

Gran let out a high pitched shriek, which scared me half to death making me jump round and round barking as I did so. She began to overbalance, falling slowly like a chopped down tree towards the table.

"Tim-ber!" called out Jimmy and Charlotte giggled.

"Catch her Harry!" shouted Mum in a panicky voice. He got there just in time and sat Gran down on a chair. Mum gave Jimmy a frown, but I noticed a slight smile at the corner of her mouth.

"What a ridiculous creature!" Gran shouted. "When did you get *this*?" She was pointing her bony finger at me.

"He's the children's birthday present," replied Mum. "They've always wanted a dog, and when we saw him in the pet shop we all fell in love with him."

"Ridiculous!" snapped Gran. "I can't believe you, Hilary, you always said you didn't like dogs! Remember that awful thing we had when you were little, it used to drive me mad, in and out of its basket all day, always wanting to be fed… and the dog hairs! Well I really can't believe it! I'm lost for words!"

It didn't sound like she was having any difficulty finding words to me! I tried again to be friendly and rested my front paws on her knees.

"GET IN YOUR BASKET!" she screeched in a shrill voice that made me go funny inside. This was when I realised that I would be having nothing to do with this person and her stick; she obviously didn't like me and I definitely didn't like *her* so far! So you can see why Gran and I don't see eye to eye and I always go and sit in my basket when I know she's on the phone… just in case.

I sat in my basket and listened as Mum talked. "Hmm," and "Oh dear…." she said as she listened to Gran. By the time Mum got off the phone Dad and the twins had planned a route for our first journey.

"Hang on a minute," said Mum, "before we get too excited, that was Gran on the phone and she's decided she wants to visit before we start chugging. It might be a few weeks until she can visit us again so I've said she can come tomorrow."

"Oh no!" groaned Dad. "We've just finished planning."

"Yes," moaned Charlotte, "the weather's going to be good tomorrow so it would be nice to have our first day of chugging in the sunshine!"

"Well I'm sure we'll have plenty more sunny days," said Mum. "Gran's getting frailer these days and we don't know how much longer she'll be able to get around and visit us, so we need to make the most of seeing her when we can."

Had I heard right? Had Mum said Gran might not be able to visit us much longer? I could only hope.

"I suppose you're right," agreed Dad. "We can always leave the day after tomorrow".

"Now, mind your head," said Dad next morning as Gran climbed grumpily down into the boat.

"Goodness me!" she huffed. "Is this how you have to get in? Walking down a ladder *backwards*?" Oh no, this wasn't a good start, she was moaning already.

"Are you alright?" asked Mum. "You've been gone ages."

"We had a bit of a drama," began Dad, but before he could continue Gran took over,

"Elsie did it!" she hissed. "She's talked about it for years but today she actually did it!"

"Did what?" asked Jimmy.

"Escaped!"

"Now hold on Dotty, she just wandered out of the building into the car park that's all," said Dad.

"She gets around pretty fast considering she's had three toes removed!" continued Gran squinting at the twins. "She had to have them off 'cos they were going bad ways!"

"Eeurgh!" said Jimmy and Charlotte together.

"Alright," interrupted Mum. "Jimmy and Charlotte, why don't you show Gran around the boat while I dish up dinner?" She looked at Dad who I could see was trying not to laugh. The tour of the boat didn't take many minutes, but Gran huffed and puffed, tutting as she went.

"Well do you like her?" asked Dad.

"Her? What do you mean her?" said Gran.

"Didn't you know Gran? All boats are girls and we always say 'her' when we talk about 'Whichwey'," said Charlotte.

"Ridiculous!" snorted Gran. "You make it sound almost human! It's only made of wood and metal you know, it's not alive!"

Gran was already putting a dampener on things and she'd only been on the boat five minutes.

After a very quiet dinner, Dad tried to brighten the atmosphere by suggesting that we go out for a short chug to let Gran see what it was like.

"Now Dotty," he said, "we can either turn right out of the marina and chug through the countryside, or go left and go through a tunnel and then down a few locks, the first of which are called staircase locks and are quite exciting. You choose." Gran chose left.

which wey

"I'll get bored otherwise," she said. "At least there'll be a bit more to see than fields of cows and sheep!"

So Dad settled Gran on a chair on the back deck, the twins helped Mum untie Whichwey, Dad started the engine and we were off.

"Why do we have to wear these awful life jackets again, Mum?" moaned Charlotte. "They look so stupid and make it difficult to move!"

"Oh come on Charlotte," Jimmy piped up, "they're not so bad, 'better safe than sorry'."

"Shut up!" shouted Charlotte. "I was speaking to Mum not you."

"Now come on Charlotte!" replied Mum. "You *know* why, we've gone over this before. The canal can be very dangerous and even though you can swim, if you fell in it could be very hard to get out. You wore them on our holiday last summer,"

"Yes but that was only for a week, I didn't think we'd have to wear them all the time now!"

Of course Gran had to have her say and started telling Charlotte to listen to her mother and not answer back, so Charlotte went off in a huff.

"You just don't discipline those children enough Hilary!" said Gran. "You would never have answered *me* back like that!"

We all stood on the back deck as we chugged off and were approaching the tunnel before we knew it. Dad switched on the light at the front of the boat but the sudden darkness was a bit scary and I let out a loud howl.

"What's the matter with the dog!" shouted Gran. She never called me by my name but always referred to me as 'The Dog!'

"He's not keen on the dark," answered Dad. "Kids! Go inside and turn all the lights on!"

The twins ran inside as I continued to howl.

"Come on, Chico," shouted Mum as she grabbed me and carried me down inside, "you stay in here, you're quite safe." As I settled in my basket I could just hear Dad say to Gran....

"You know this tunnel is supposed to be haunted." Ooh, that made me shiver! We chugged deeper and deeper into the darkness and the engine seemed to roar louder as it echoed off the walls. The brickwork in the tunnel ran with water and every so often large drips fell from the ceiling onto the boat. Well I bet you've guessed Gran's reaction? Yes, she moaned and moaned!

"It's so cold...! I'm getting wet...! Mind out! Don't drive so close to the walls!" It went on and on. Jimmy and Charlotte found it really exciting and kept squealing and shouting to hear how their voices echoed. They even made wailing ghost sounds to see if they could scare Gran, but it was too dark to see each other's faces so it was difficult to tell if it worked. I stayed inside the boat, it was too wet for me, I preferred being curled up in my basket.

The tunnel was quite long and the twenty minutes it took to chug through it seemed to go on forever. At last we were back out in the warm sunshine and Gran actually stopped complaining and looked quite content to sit back and watch the fields go by. I went and sat back up at the front with Jimmy and Charlotte on the little bench seats.

The children enjoyed seeing all the ducks and their ducklings. The ducklings were quite big now, but still kept very close to their mothers. We passed a field of sheep, who all looked up at once as the boat went by, then a field of cows, with some of them balancing on the edge of the bank trying to get a drink from the canal.

It was lovely and peaceful and everyone was starting to relax in the warm sunshine. Charlotte took some photographs and I was just was beginning to nod off when Dad shouted,

"Here are the locks!" He steered the boat towards the bank and Jimmy, Charlotte and Mum carefully stepped off holding their windlasses.

I wasn't worried at all about locks. We'd been through one last summer at a place called Sutton Stop and, whilst the twins had enjoyed helping to open and close the gates and having a go at turning the windlass, the whole process hadn't seemed to achieve much as the level of the canal before the lock was almost the same as the level after it. The lock we were approaching now looked very different, the gates were much bigger than I remembered and even from where I was sitting I could see, as the boat nosed slowly into the lock, that the level of the canal dropped alarmingly on the other side.

These locks were taking the canal downhill which meant that when the boat was inside and the gates had been closed behind it, the children would wind up the paddles on the bottom gates to release the water into the lower level of the canal. As the water level dropped, the boat would go down with it until it was level with the canal ahead of us, then we could open the front gates and go forward. This was nothing like Sutton Stop, it looked such a long way down! Just then the twins used their windlasses to crank open the paddles. There was an enormous roaring whooshing sound and the water below the gates began to bubble and swirl with powerful currents. Slowly the boat moved downwards leaving the walls of the lock dripping with water. I felt quite safe on the boat and it was very exciting!

I could only imagine what Gran was saying now, I could hear the drone of her distant voice, and was sure Dad was getting moaned at for all the dripping water.

The next three locks were staircase locks. This is where there is no gap in between each lock and they go down like a stepladder. These were a little more complicated to use and a man called a 'lock keeper' helped boaters get by safely. He told the children his name was Terry and I watched as the twins chatted away to him telling him how they lived aboard. Even Charlotte was starting to sound enthusiastic.

"Lucky you!" Terry said. "I bet you'll have lots of adventures."

He didn't realise how right he was and the first one was literally just around the corner! As we chugged out of the third lock in the staircase and the children waved goodbye to Terry, I noticed there was another one a little further ahead. Mum was already opening the gates. I decided that I'd had enough of watching from the boat and would rather join the twins and Mum. Dad had steered the boat towards the side to let a boat pass and just as he was pulling away again, I leapt for the bank.

I quickly discovered that I wasn't quite as good at jumping as I thought.

This is when it all became a bit of a blur...

I missed the bank completely and belly-flopped into the canal! Dad hadn't seen me nor had Mum or the twins, but Gran had. She was so shocked that she attempted to stand up without the aid of her stick. Well, this was a mistake. As she shouted,

"Harry, the dog!" she overbalanced and knocked the chair she had been sitting on into the canal. There was a big splash and Dad panicked trying to catch Gran, rescue the chair and steer the boat all at the same time! In the meantime I was doggy paddling like mad trying to get out of the way of the boat which was getting closer and closer.

As she got herself up Gran was shouting at Dad and pointing frantically,

"THE DOG, THE DOG! He's in the water!" At this point all eyes were turned on me. Mum ran to me, reached out, grabbed my collar and pulled me on to the bank just as Dad managed to stop the boat. Phew, that was close!

I'd never been so scared. Dad tied the boat up and Mum carried me back on board looking a bit tearful. The twins rushed up to me hugging and patting me until I thought I would suffocate. Dad fetched a towel to wrap me up in and dry me off and even Gran looked relieved that I was safe. Perhaps I'd misjudged her after all. Well, let's face it, it was Gran who had really saved me, if she hadn't had seen me and alerted the others I dread to think what might have happened!

When we had all calmed down a bit Dad rescued the chair out of the water and I finally stopped shaking. Charlotte finally agreed that she could now see why it was important she and Jimmy always wore their lifejackets in the future. After one more lock going down we turned Whichwey around and headed back towards our marina. I decided to stay inside for the return journey.

During the chug home Dad told us that you could get life jackets for dogs and that they'd buy me one at the next Chandlers we came to.

"He'll be much safer, the jacket will keep him afloat and they have handles, so it will be easier to grab him if he does fall in again," said Dad.

"What's a Chandlers?" asked Jimmy.

"A Chandlers is a shop that sells all sorts of things that you need if you have a boat. Things like ropes, fenders, windlasses, ooh, all kinds of useful stuff," replied Dad. "You'll see for yourself tomorrow."

When we got back to the marina Mum made a cup of tea and cut some slices of cake for everyone and we all sat quietly munching and drinking, beginning to appreciate that life afloat was going to be very different. Gran was looking quite pleased with herself as she sat slurping her tea. I think she'd rather enjoyed herself though she couldn't quite bring herself to say so. Dad took her back to the home and when he got back told us how she'd retold the story of my little adventure over and over again to whoever would listen, stressing how *she'd* been the hero of the day!

Well, what a day we'd had. Who'd have guessed the first adventure on the boat would be all about me! I surely wouldn't have!

CHAPTER FOUR

excitement at the chandlers

The next day we set off early as Dad said it would take us quite a few hours to get to the Chandlers. We waved goodbye to Michele and Henri in the sales office as we chugged out of the marina.

michele ↘

"Have fun!" Henri barked. "When you 'ave returned you will tell me about your adventures? Oui?"

I was relieved I was getting a lifejacket. I didn't think I would ever forget falling in and didn't relish the thought of it happening again. We had to chug the same way as we had the day before, but this time I stayed inside the boat through Crick tunnel and the locks.

A little while after the locks we came to Norton Junction and turned right, heading for a place called Braunston.

"There's a nice pub called 'The Boat' just before the Chandlers," said Dad, "so we could stop and have lunch before we go and buy Chico's jacket."

We chugged along and the pretty countryside passed slowly by. I came up onto the front deck with Charlotte and Jimmy, while Mum and Dad were on the back, Dad steering and Mum studying the map. Only half an hour had passed and I was starting to relax when Mum shouted,

"Kids come and help me put all the lights on, here comes another tunnel!"

Oh no, not another one! Two tunnels in one day was too much for me, I ran inside and curled up in my basket.

This tunnel seemed to go on and on, it was much longer than the other one. The children kept squealing as the water poured onto the boat from the ceiling above.

"I'm not sure I like this tunnel," said Mum shivering, as we got deeper into it. "You can't see the other end and it's much colder than the one at Crick. I wonder if this one is haunted too?"

Finally we could see daylight and emerged into the bright, warm sunshine and guess what I saw ahead after we had chugged for five minutes? Yes you guessed it, more locks! This time the map showed us that there were six double width locks quite close together.

"Great!" said Dad, "two boats are just coming out and there's a boat waiting so we can share the work and go down with them."

There was a family with two children on the other boat. I could hear lots of chattering as the twins excitedly told the other family that we *lived* on our boat and how they wouldn't have to go to school anymore.

The other family had just hired their boat for a couple of days. The two children looked similar ages to Jimmy and Charlotte and told them their names were Beth and George and that they had never done locks before. The twins were delighted to hear this and enjoyed explaining how they worked. They showed Beth and George what to do and Mum took some photos of them all pushing as hard as they could against the balance beams to swing the heavy gates open and closed.

Charlotte seemed to enjoy talking to Beth. I could hear her talking about how she didn't want to live on a boat to start with, but was getting used to it now. She went on to say it was lovely to see Mum and Dad so happy, but that she was still a little worried about the home tutoring Mum and Dad were planning when school restarted. Beth said she thought that could be fun.

After a while, I decided to go and sit on the front deck, making sure I wasn't too near the edge. As I settled down, I heard a whimpering sound from the boat next to us and looked across to see a little white poodle with a red bow on her head shaking in a basket on the front deck.

"What's wrong?" I asked.

"I'm scared!" she whimpered in a shaky voice. "I don't like the look of these locks and I'm only just getting over the shock of that dreadful tunnel! I didn't like all the noise and drips of water."

I felt really sorry for her.

"Don't worry," I replied, "I didn't like the tunnel either and after what happened yesterday I stay in my basket when we go through locks."

"Why, what happened yesterday?" she enquired. Now, I confess I got a bit carried away telling my story!

"Well, when we were just in between two locks I decided I wanted to go on the bank with the children," I began. "I had to jump from the edge of the boat, but the bank was further away than I realised and..." I paused here to make it more exciting, "I landed in the water!"

The poodle's eyes opened wide and she looked even more scared.

"I couldn't get up onto the bank because it was so slippery. I barked and barked, but no one could hear me!" By now she was shaking even more and I was enjoying the way my story sounded so exciting. I added details as I went along, describing the coldness of the water, the roaring of the boat engine getting closer to me as Dad swung the boat around to go into the lock, the screams from Gran as the chair fell into the water. By the time I'd finished the poor little thing was quivering from head to tail. All at once I realised how mean I'd been scaring her so much and felt a bit guilty; it had been scary, but I'd made it sound much worse than it was.

"Oh, it all ended up okay." I laughed. "Gran was a hero because she noticed I'd fallen in and after they'd made sure I was alright I was completely spoilt for the rest of the day!"

The little poodle looked quite relieved and a little calmer but her front legs still shook ever so slightly. We sat in silence for a while as the boats came down the first four locks and with two more to go I tried to distract my new friend by starting up the conversation again.

I learned that her name was Flossy and that she was two years old. She had lived with her owners since she was a puppy and was fairly happy, although she was often lonely as her owners were all out during weekdays at work and school.

I told her how it had been the same in my family, but that now we were always together.

She listened and said how lovely it must be not to be on your own all the time.

After chugging past Braunston Marina we found two moorings right outside the pub. Dad had already told the other family about the pub and they decided to stop and have lunch as well.

We sat outside looking across the canal. It was such a lovely day. The warm afternoon sun shone through the trees and sparkled on the water. While our families laughed and chatted telling each other about the funny things that had happened to them on their boats, Flossy and I lay on the floor snoozing in the afternoon sun.

Suddenly I could smell a delicious smell. Was it? Yes, it was DINNER! The waitress was bringing everyone's food, chicken, steak, meat pies, burgers and chips. Yum I could eat any of those!

"What's your favourite food, Flossy?" I asked her.

"Oh… I have to be careful what I eat as I'm wheat and lactose intolerant," replied Flossy.

I had no idea what she was on about.

"I only eat special biscuits my owners get me, they are very healthy but don't taste of much."

I was speechless which is unusual for me! Poor Flossy! I couldn't bear it if that was all I could eat. Just when I was thinking how thirsty I was, Dad put down a dish full of beer for me.

"Oh Harry, don't give Chico beer!" said Mum. "You know how it makes him even more silly than usual and if he falls asleep it always makes him snore."

Excuse me, had I heard right? Silly? Me? What could Mum have meant? I know things seemed to happen around me, but not because I was silly, just because… well… just because.

Snore? I didn't snore! Dad snored, I'd heard him only the other night, but me? I decided to drink the beer quickly, worried that Mum would take it away. I positioned myself next to Dad's legs giving him big puppy eyes, which meant 'I'm hungry, p-l-e-a-s-e give me some of your dinner!' When Mum wasn't looking he slipped me the odd chip and I even got a bit of his steak.

When Mum took the children inside to the toilet Dad refilled my bowl with beer.

"Look Flossy." I said, "try some of this, it's lovely!" Flossy looked a bit apprehensive, but I think she must have been thirsty because once she started to lap it up she got carried away and finished the lot!

"Gosh Flossy, You were thirsty!" I said, a little disappointed that I hadn't had a look in.

When Mum and the children returned it was time for dessert. Now this really was my favourite. I love ice cream, especially chocolate and Jimmy had ordered an enormous chocolate sundae covered in chocolate sauce and sprinkles.

Now it was Jimmy's turn to get my attention. I sat by him and did big puppy eyes again. Jimmy noticed and lifted out a large blob of ice cream on the end of his finger. I licked it off quickly before Mum could see.

"I saw that!" warned Mum. "You and your dad are as bad as each other. I'm surprised Chico's not fatter than he is with all the rubbish you give him."

'Fatter?' I was beginning to feel Mum was being rather mean to me today. First I was 'silly' and 'snored', now I was 'fatter!'

I decided to go and sit back by Flossy. She was lying fast asleep again… and was that snoring I could hear?

I must have nodded off as well because the next thing I heard was Dad.

"Come on!" he shouted, waking us up with a start. "We're all going to the Chandlers and you, Chico, need a lifejacket."

The Chandlers was just along the road from the pub so we all followed Dad, including Flossy and her family whom I'd discovered were called the 'Joneses.' They had decided to buy Flossy a lifejacket as well.

"It might make her more confident on the boat," Mr Jones had said. "It's such a shame she's so nervous she's really missing out on the fun!"

We walked into the Chandlers to find it very busy.

"Oh look, over there," said Dad standing on tiptoe to see through the bustle and he led the way to a shelf piled high with bright orange life jackets. "I wonder which one would be best?"

He looked around for a sales assistant, but they were all busy and he couldn't see anyone who could help us.

"Let's just wait, Harry," suggested Mum. "We really *do* need some advice, let's wait for someone to come free."

Before Mum had finished what she was saying Dad had already pulled two or three life jackets from the pile.

"Don't be so impatient!" hissed Mum, trying not to raise her voice too high. But would Dad listen?

I found myself being picked up by Dad. He was trying to put something dark over my head and I found I couldn't see.

This was when it all became a bit of blur…

A suffocating feeling came over me and I started to struggle and felt like I couldn't breathe.

"Keep still, Chico, you silly dog!" pleaded Dad, but I couldn't. I started to get panicky and the more Dad pulled the thing over my head, the worse it got.

Suddenly I wriggled out of Dad's hands completely and fell heavily to the floor. Still in the dark and feeling dizzy I started running round and round, shaking my head and bumping into things. I tried to bark but couldn't make a sound. Then with one sudden jerk I was free... or so I thought!

By now Dad had started to chase me around the shop with an audience of shop assistants and customers silently staring, unable to believe the pandemonium that was developing. As I ran around trying to shake off something that seemed to be caught on my collar, I knocked over a display of shoes that had been neatly placed on shelves. With shoes tumbling all over the floor I shook my head and in doing so the thing that was caught on my collar, it turned out to be the lifejacket, flew off into a tall pile of toilet rolls that had been neatly stacked. Dozens of toilet rolls came tumbling down and were rolling all over the floor, people looked like they were dancing as they tried not to stand on them.

"Come here, Chico!" shouted the twins, as they ran after me. By now there were shouts and running feet in all directions as staff and customers alike gave chase. With all the rumpus, Flossy, who is, as we know, a nervous dog, had also started to panic. She joined in, running around yapping madly and knocking more things over as she went.

Suddenly I felt myself being grabbed and lifted into the air. Twisting around to see who it was I met the eyes of a very angry shop assistant. I stopped barking and struggling. I noticed that another shop assistant had picked up Flossy in the same way, but she was still barking and shaking all over.

Next we found ourselves deposited outside the shop. As the two shop assistants turned around and returned to the shop they shouted, "AND STAY THERE!"

By now the twins and George and Beth were outside cuddling us both.

"Oh, Chico, are you alright?" cried Charlotte. "You silly dog, Dad was only trying to put the lifejacket on you."

Well if that's what lifejackets were like I wasn't sure I wanted one any more!

After everything had calmed down and Mum and Dad had helped to tidy up the mess, a shop assistant explained that the jacket Dad was trying on me was too small. Rather than let me back into the shop the assistants agreed that he could bring jackets outside for me to try on.

chico in his lifejacket

We left the Chandlers quickly after finding one that went comfortably over my head and fitted perfectly.

Flossy was still in such a state that the Jones's decided they wouldn't even try to put a jacket on her, they were nearing the end of their holiday anyway.

That night Mum was still a little cross with Dad, blaming him for what had happened, so the twins tried to lighten the atmosphere by suggesting we decorate their jackets and mine using felt tip pens. By the time we went to bed everyone was happy again, including me, although I kept a wary eye on the now colourful life jacket that was hanging up next to my basket. I wondered how many more adventures I would have while I was wearing it.

CHAPTER FIVE

duck chasing

After Braunston we continued up the Oxford Canal. Flossy and her owners followed behind us. We left early because they were dropping off their rental boat before midday at a yard called Clifton Cruisers, which is situated just after the next locks at Hillmorton. These are not double locks but two single locks next to each other and as there was nothing coming the other way we could still travel down together. Flossy wasn't looking so good.

"What's wrong with you?" I asked.

"I'm not sure if I had too much sun yesterday," she replied.

"I've been feeling rather queasy and I've got a bit of a headache."

Hmm I thought, remembering how quickly my beer had disappeared, I don't think it was too much sun!

"I bet you slept well last night though didn't you?"

"You know, thinking back on it, I did." Answered Flossy as I chuckled to myself. She was still a little nervous as we entered the locks, whereas I was feeling much more confident wearing my colourful lifejacket.

Mum was driving today and Dad was doing the locks with Jimmy. Charlotte was sitting in the front with me. As we moved into the first lock I wasn't sure if it was my imagination, but was Mum driving a little too fast?

We soon found out she was as the boat rammed into the front gates of the lock! Charlotte shouted for Mum to stop and I barked furiously. We hit the gates with a loud BANG!

"Sorry!" shouted Mum. "I couldn't see how close we were to the gates it's really difficult to judge at the back here! Whichwey's much longer than the boat we rented last summer."

"Crikey," said Charlotte, "I thought we were going to go right through those lock doors!"

After the first lock we chugged on a little way towards the next one. This time I hoped Mum would manoeuvre more slowly, but no, she did the same thing again. Charlotte was standing up and waving her arms and shouting at Mum to warn her to stop, but she wasn't quite tall enough for Mum to see. This time we hit with such a bump that a loud crash came from inside the boat. I rushed inside to see Mum's favourite vase smashed on the floor. The impact from hitting the gates had made it fall off the shelf.

"Oh no! Sorry!" shouted Mum again. "I don't think I'm very good at this! Maybe you should drive into locks in future Harry."

"Mum can't always do the locks Chico, she will get too tired," said Charlotte looking at me. "What we need is a way to let Mum know when to stop inside a lock. I wonder how we could do that?" I had absolutely no idea, but knowing Jimmy and Charlotte I was sure that they would come up with something.

We chugged slowly past a little café and Charlotte waved to the people who were watching the boats going into the last lock. This was when Mum insisted Dad took over, she didn't want to embarrass herself with people watching. I was relieved and Charlotte looked more relaxed as we glided slowly and accurately into the lock.

After the bottom lock we said goodbye to Flossy and her family, the children swapped email addresses and promised to keep in touch.

Half an hour later we approached Clifton Cruisers.

"Let us know what adventures you have," Shouted Beth and George as we chugged past them. Their parents waved and shouted more goodbyes while I barked to Flossy hoping I would see her again one day.

We carried on chugging and passed through Rugby where, thank goodness, there were no more locks. Jimmy had joined me and Charlotte at the front of the boat and Charlotte was telling him how Mum struggled driving the boat into locks.

"We really must come up with a way to let Mum know when she needs to stop," said Charlotte. "She's going to have to drive the boat into locks again sometime or other. She can't always open and close the lock gates, it's such hard work and she's already got a bad back!" Jimmy agreed.

"But what can we do? She didn't see you waving did she? We need to come up with another idea. I know, I'll ask Mum what she thinks."

"No!" Insisted Charlotte. "Don't do that, she'll only get upset. She's already cross with herself as it is."

"Oh alright," conceded Jimmy. "I suppose you're right, we don't want to upset her, but we've got to do something."

We arrived at our next mooring about teatime. It was a small boatyard called Lime Farm Marina just after bridge forty-two. This is where we had rented our boat from last summer. It was run by a friendly couple called John and Sarah. Mum and Dad had become friends with them and kept in touch after the holiday. Sarah and John had lots of dogs, one of which was a Jack Russell just like me, called 'Scrappy'.

Scrappy was a real rufty-tufty boat dog and I couldn't wait to see him again. He was confident and lively, always wanting people to throw sticks for him which he would bring back and then refuse to let go.

"Keeps them on their toes!" he'd say. "They get bored if I drop it without a tug of war first."

← scrappy

Sure enough, there was Scrappy waiting for us with a puzzled look on his face. I jumped off the boat and we rushed to greet each other.

"What on earth is that?" he exclaimed. I realised he meant my lifejacket. "You look like a cushion with legs!"

"What a cheek!" I replied indignantly.

"I'll have you know that this is the latest in dog safety wear!"

"The ducks and swans round here will laugh at you, just you wait and see!" chuckled Scrappy.

I decided I had better explain why I had a lifejacket on. I retold my adventure of falling into the canal once again, making it sound even more dramatic than when I had told Flossy. Scrappy just gave me a look as if to say, 'Soft! That's what you are!'

John and Sarah admired our boat and insisted we stay for a few days. Sarah kindly offered to take Mum shopping, so it was arranged that the next day the twins and Mum would go shopping with Sarah while Dad would stay with John, who was mending a boat engine. Dad said he was fine staying behind,

"There are a few jobs I need to do anyway," he told us, "so don't rush back on my account."

Scrappy had insisted we go and tease the ducks. Now Scrappy wasn't fond of ducks though he'd never told me why and he liked to chase them whenever he could. He would creep up behind them quietly so that they wouldn't notice, then when he was really close he would start barking madly. The ducks would be so startled that they'd quack furiously and flap their wings trying to half run and half fly to get away. Scrappy would continue to chase them barking as he went. It was a spectacular thing to see and hear!

As Scrappy prepared to chase two ducks that were waddling close by I spotted two white ones walking along by the bridge. They looked bigger than the ones Scrappy was after and I wanted to show him I was tough, so without saying a word I ran towards them.

I could hear Scrappy barking madly. What was he doing? Trying to scare *my* ducks away no doubt, well, I'd show him!

careful chico↗

I slowed down as I approached them, they seemed a lot bigger close up and my confidence started to leave me, but no! If Scrappy could do it then so could I. I wasn't going to let him think I was scared, he'd already laughed at my lifejacket and I wasn't going to have him laughing at my attempt at duck chasing. As I crept up behind the two white ducks they didn't move at all. I was almost on top of them, oh, it was so scary but exciting! I was crouching on my tummy behind the larger of the two and was taking a deep breath so I could bark really loudly when it, very slowly, turned around and its beady black eyes stared straight into mine.

This is when it all became a bit of a blur...

I tried hard to bark but nothing would come out. Its long yellow beak was almost touching my nose and it wasn't looking scared at all. I, however, was having second thoughts about the whole thing and could feel my legs shaking. Suddenly it opened its beak, stuck out its tongue and hissed loudly! I closed my eyes, felt a sharp stab on the end of my nose and then a great whoosh! Something hit me and I found myself rolling over and over until with a big splash, yes you've guessed it, I fell in the canal again! I had no idea ducks were so strong!

I was a bit dizzy but found it really easy to stay afloat. Thank goodness for my lifejacket!

By now Scrappy was barking madly and Dad and John had rushed out to see what all the kerfuffle was. The white ducks were still flapping about wildly and I wasn't sure, but was that laughter I could hear as they pointed their wings at me? Scrappy barked and charged at them.

"Scrappy! Get away from those swans!" shouted John. Swans...? Oh... they weren't ducks then?

"Hold on Chico!" shouted Dad as he came running towards me. This time I wasn't panicking, I felt quite safe in my lifejacket. He pulled me out of the water and stood me back on dry land. Scrappy came running over,

"Didn't you hear me barking for you to come away?" he shouted. "You never, NEVER annoy swans! That's the first thing you learn! Didn't anyone ever tell you?"

Vague memories came back to me from last summer when we had our holiday on the canal.

"Oh yes, now I remember," I said. "Jimmy told me last year to keep away from the swans or I'd be sorry. I didn't know what a swan looked like and I wasn't sure what I'd be sorry about, but now I get it!"

Scrappy rolled his eyes at me and stood there shaking his head. I was feeling rather silly, as if I'd let him down a bit but as I looked at him more closely I saw something I hadn't noticed before. He had three scars on his nose... perhaps Scrappy had learned about swans the hard way too!

When Mum and the twins came back from their shopping trip they were surprised to see me and Scrappy quietly snoozing in the shade of a tree.

"What's wrong with you two?" asked Charlotte. "I thought you'd be chasing the ducks all afternoon!"

"Oh, don't worry they have been," chipped in Dad, "and Chico got a lesson in telling the difference between swans and ducks!"

"Oh Chico, what have you been up to now?" said Jimmy as Dad proceeded to tell them all about it.

"What did I tell you Chico? I don't think you'll try that again will you?"

And you know what? I never did!

The next morning Jimmy and Charlotte were sitting at the front of the boat talking in whispers with Dad. What were they up to? I never liked to be left out of anything so I went and sat on Dad's lap.

"What are you after Chico?" said Dad, so I licked his face and nuzzled into his neck. "Oh okay then, you can stay here as long as you sit quietly!"

I discovered the twins were telling Dad about how Mum was really struggling to know when to stop when she was steering the boat into a lock. They were concerned that not only was she damaging the boat with the bumps, but the bumps could make me, yes *me* Chico, fall overboard and into the water. Oh, I hadn't thought of it like that, my goodness what would I do if I fell into a lock?

It was dangerous even wearing a lifejacket, because I could get squashed between the boat and the lock walls! I could feel myself trembling just thinking about it.

"Don't worry, Chico," said Dad soothingly, "the twins are going to design something that will help."

While Dad went off to make Mum a cup of tea the twins got out their pens and paper. I sat with them watching as they drew and chatted sharing ideas.

After about an hour they showed Dad what they had drawn. There were two flags one blue and one yellow.

"What are they for?" asked Dad.

"Well," Jimmy explained, "we thought we could sit at the front of the boat and wave a blue flag at Mum as she drives into the locks, blue meaning 'Go'. Then when she needs to stop, wave the yellow flag."

"That was Jimmy's idea," said Charlotte, "but I'm not sure if Mum will be able to see them that clearly and what if we lose the flags?"

Jimmy continued, pointing to the picture of a bell.

"Then I thought about ringing a bell to warn her when to stop."

"But we know how noisy the engine is," said Charlotte. "Mum might not be able to hear it."

Jimmy frowned as Charlotte dismissed all of *his* ideas. Dad pointed to a design of lines and little light bulbs.

"This looks interesting," he commented.

"Yes this is our favourite design," smiled Charlotte sweetly. "It's mine."

Jimmy sighed and rolled his eyes.

"You see I tried to think of what makes people stop when they are driving a car," Charlotte continued. "Then I remembered traffic lights and what green and red lights mean.

If we made some lights like that we could warn Mum when to stop."

"Well you've got some great ideas!" said Dad. "What will you need for the lights?"

Then Charlotte showed Dad her labeled design.

"When we made a circuit in school," she said, "we used wires, bulbs, switches, and batteries."

Where were they going to get all these things?

"Can we get them from the Chandlers?" asked Jimmy.

"No, I've got a better idea," said Dad. "I know we've got all these things on the boat, so why don't you two show just how clever you are and see if you can make it by yourselves!"

Now the twins looked puzzled. We had all these things already on the boat? I hadn't seen them and the twins looked confused so it didn't look as if they knew where to find them either. Dad walked away with a grin on his face. He was enjoying this!

As the twins chatted away trying to think where they would find batteries and light bulbs, I spotted Jimmy's torch poking out from under his pillow. I remembered that Jimmy used this at night so he could see to read his book before he went to sleep. Charlotte always moaned if he kept the light on. Yes, the torch might help I thought, I just had to make the twins see it. I started to bark, and scratch with my paws at Jimmy's pillow.

"What are you doing you silly dog!" shouted Jimmy. "Come away from my bed! You're not getting in there!"
As he came over and pulled me away the torch fell onto the floor.

"Hey Chico you clever thing!" he exclaimed. "You were trying to show us the torch weren't you?"

"Oh Chico you're so clever!" said Charlotte.

"A torch has a bulb and batteries, just what we needed."

Oh… had it got those things? I hadn't realised! All I knew was that light shone out of the end. Still I wagged my tail showing I was happy to help and gave a confident look as if to say 'Of course I knew!'

"I'm sure I've seen some wire in Dad's tool box," said Jimmy, "so we've got everything we need!"

"Lunch is ready." called Mum. "What are you two up to?" "Nothing!" the twins chorused together.

After lunch they worked away using light bulbs and batteries from other torches they had. Dad had a switch in his toolbox too and Charlotte came up with the great idea of using cellophane sweet wrappers to make the lights look red or green.

When they had finished they showed it proudly to Mum and Dad.

"Wow, that's fantastic!" said Mum. "Do you know what you have just been doing?"

Other than having fun the children didn't know what she meant.

"You've been doing a science investigation! Well done!" "You know school restarts in a couple of weeks?" reminded Mum.

Both the twins were well aware of this, but Jimmy was happier about it than Charlotte.

"Well it doesn't mean you'll miss out on lessons you know! You'll be doing literacy every day with me and numeracy every day with Dad!"

"Oh no," groaned Jimmy. "Will we have to do work every day?"

"Yes, I'm afraid so,' said Mum, "but just look at the fun you've had today.

You didn't even realise you were doing science until I pointed it out, did you? Well Dad and I will try to make all lessons fun. In fact, how about you start now by keeping a diary? It will be a good record of what we've been doing and will help you practise your writing."

Both twins were smiling, this didn't sound so bad after all. It sounded great to me! I liked the idea that they would be writing about all the things we were doing together, I wondered if they would mention me and the adventures I'd had already. I hoped so!

CHAPTER
SIX

party time

We stayed with John and Sarah for a few days. When we left they came to wave goodbye to us as we chugged off. Scrappy stood quietly on the bank. I think he was secretly going to miss me, even though, knowing Scrappy, he would never admit it.

We turned left out of the marina to carry on up the Oxford canal.

"We have to be in Coventry for Saturday night," explained Dad. "Pete's just phoned me to say we've got a gig at a club in town." Pete was the guitarist in Dad's band and they often shared lifts.

"Oh that's good," said Mum. "You could walk to the gig from the canal basin, but how will you get all your gear there?"

"Don't worry," replied Dad. "Pete's offered to pick me up, he wants to see the boat anyway."

Our lives started to settle into a comfortable routine on the boat. We would chug for one or two hours a day, sometimes more if it was sunny. Other days we wouldn't chug at all if we found a nice place to stop.

It had taken us about a week to reach Sutton Stop, the place where we'd first seen a lock last year. After reading the map Dad suggested we moor just before the pub. The pub was called 'The Greyhound,' it was right on Sutton Stop junction and we remembered it did great food. Mum suggested we stay there for a couple of days as the weather had turned wet. Everyone agreed. That's one thing we'd discovered on a narrowboat: it's not half so much fun steering and doing locks in the rain!

On the second evening the weather was starting to look more cheerful.

We sat outside 'The Greyhound' having dinner and Mum brought up the subject of the children's birthday.

"Now what are we going to do for your birthdays next Saturday?" said Mum.

"Well we can't have a party this year can we?" replied Charlotte with a sullen look on her face. "None of our friends would come."

"Now, hang on a minute," said Dad. "Of course they would. We're going to be moored in Coventry over the next few days and that's not too far for any of your friends."

"Yes, of course," said Mum enthusiastically. "And we could go shopping in town to buy everything we'll need for the party!"

"That's great," said Charlotte. "So we could have a party after all!"

"Have you thought about inviting Gran?" asked Dad. "She's always come to your birthday parties in the past and she'd be so upset if she found out how close we were and hadn't invited her!"

Oh no! What was Dad saying? Gran *wasn't* expecting an invite! We had already told her that this year we would be chugging for Jimmy and Charlotte's birthdays. Now was Dad going to make us feel guilty if she didn't come?

"Oh … do we have to?" whined Jimmy. "She always moans about our friends. She says they're too noisy and all my friends are scared of her!"

"Yes," said Charlotte, agreeing with Jimmy for once. "Last year at our party, she shouted at Emily and made her cry! Then Emily wanted to go home early."

"Now, you two, don't exaggerate," replied Mum. "We all know Gran isn't so keen on noise, but that's because she's getting older and it mithers her.

I'm sure she'll make more effort to be cheerful now that she doesn't see so much of us." I wasn't so sure and by the looks on the twins' faces I could see that they weren't either.

"Oh… alright," replied a less than enthusiastic Jimmy. "Perhaps if we give her something to do to keep her busy she won't notice if our friends get noisy."

"I know," said Charlotte enthusiastically, "she could watch Chico for us. We don't want him getting into any more mischief! Remember the last time Gran was on the boat, she helped save him from drowning. I think Gran actually likes Chico more these days. In fact," Charlotte continued, tickling me under the chin, "I think you might even say she's getting quite fond of you." I gave her one of my 'Oh dear' looks.

'Liking me?' 'Fond of me?' Who was Charlotte kidding? She just wanted Gran out of her way and I had drawn the short straw! It wouldn't be Gran looking after me, it would be me looking after Gran! Oh great… I couldn't wait.

"I know, let's set off first thing in the morning and see what it's like," suggested Dad, "that will give us plenty of time to plan the party. First though you know what you two have got to do? Send invitations."

"Oh bother!" moaned Charlotte. "We forgot about that. We'd have to make them and then find a post box. I don't think we've got enough time!"

"Hang on a minute!" shouted Jimmy. "I know what we could do, we could design an invitation on the computer and then email it to all our friends."

"What a great idea! Jimmy you're so clever!" said Charlotte. Jimmy couldn't believe it! Had Charlotte said he was clever?

"Thanks Charlie," he replied quietly.

Charlotte stopped.

"Did you just call me 'Charlie'?" she asked, looking surprised. "You know, I quite like that... Hmm, Charlie... Yes I do like it! Right, everyone listen! I've changed my name!" she announced. "Everyone's got to call me Charlie from now on."

"I think it really suits you," said Dad grinning. "Charlie it is then."

The next day the children were excited because they could try out their new science invention on Mum. About fifty metres from where they had moored, just before the pub, was the very shallow lock they had been through last year. It had been put there over one hundred years ago to stop boats so that they could be charged to use the rest of the canal.

"It's a bit like the toll road we use sometimes when we go to Birmingham," Dad told the children. "You don't have to pay at this one anymore though."

The children thought it would be a good lock for Mum to practise on, so they set up the red and green lights at the front of the boat in a place where Mum could see them.

Mum drove carefully into the lock and as the boat got closer to the lock gates Jimmy switched the light from green to red. We all held our breaths waiting for the bang, but no... Mum stopped the boat gently just in front of the gates.

"Those lights are great!" she shouted to the twins. "See, I can do it now!"

Phew! We were all pleased and breathed a sigh of relief. Charlie and Jimmy's invention had worked!

We arrived at Coventry basin about teatime and Jimmy and Charlie designed and emailed all their invitations. Charlie made sure she invited Emily as she had really missed her and of course Jimmy invited Marc. They even invited Beth and George and told them to bring Flossy as well.

FROM jimmy and charlie chugg
TO emily,marc,beth,george
SUBJECT party time

YOU ARE
INVITED TO

jimmy
and
charlie's

BIRTHDAY
PARTY

reply

The next day they planned their party right down to the balloons and birthday cake and walked into town to buy everything they needed.

"You stay here Chico," Mum said as they left. "It'll be too busy in town for you and we've got a lot of shopping to do. "Don't worry," she continued as she noticed my sad expression, "we won't be long and I promise we'll take you for a walk as soon as we get back."

They actually didn't seem to be away too long before Jimmy and Charlie bounded back onto the boat. They had bags brimming with goodies and were chatting about how they were going to make hats for their party.

"Oh no!" said a weary Mum when they got back. "You know what we forgot to buy? The birthday cake!"

"Oh don't worry," said Dad, "we'll have to go back into town again tomorrow kids. OK?"

"Hooray!" replied the twins at the same time. They had enjoyed being back in town looking around all the shops.

"Can we go to the Herbert Museum tomorrow then?" asked Jimmy. "It's been ages since we went there."

"No, I'm the eldest!" shouted Charlie. "I say we go shopping! I'd like a new top for our party!"

Of course an argument ensued.

"Now wait a minute you two!" said Dad. "We've got time to do both so stop arguing!"

Much to Dad's amazement the children stopped.

"OK," they both said together and walked off discussing how they were going to decorate the boat.

Dad looked at me.

"Good grief Chico, did that really just happen? Jimmy and Charlie agreeing? Come on let's go for a walk."

Yep, things were beginning to change around here and definitely for the better!

The next morning was the day before the birthday party and Dad took Jimmy and Charlie back into town to get the cake. Mum stayed on the boat with me making food for the party and it was quite late in the afternoon when they got back. They spent the rest of the day decorating the inside of the boat, while Mum carried on cooking.

I decided I might as well accept that everyone was too busy for me at the moment so I kept out of everyone's way and stayed in my basket. Just as I was beginning to doze off, the twins suddenly grabbed me.

"Come on Chico. Did you think we'd forgotten you?" The twins gave me a big cuddle and tickled me on my tummy. So they hadn't forgotten me? I was feeling very pleased until I realised what they wanted to do. Charlie and Jimmy had been making party hats for all their friends and had decided I needed one too. So before I knew it they were pulling some sort of string under my chin and trying to put something on my head! I started to feel the same panic that I'd had when Dad tried to put the lifejacket on me a few weeks ago. Oh no, was it going to be one of those 'Bit of a blur' moments again?

"Stop you two!" shouted Dad. "Can't you see he doesn't like it?"

Dad took the hat off me just as I was starting to bark and throw myself about. Thank goodness, he was just in time. I wouldn't have liked a repeat performance of that afternoon at the Chandlers.

I decided perhaps it was better if everyone *did* just ignore me, it was certainly safer, so I went back to my basket and stayed there quietly for the rest of the day.

The next day was their birthday and Jimmy and Charlie were up early. Mum and Dad had bought them both fishing rods with all the bits and pieces they would need.

"Wow, GREAT!" they both shouted.

"Now we can go fishing with you like you promised Dad!" said Jimmy. "And we've got our *own* rods!" I couldn't believe it! This time last year they'd have moaned if they'd have been given a present like that, they'd have wanted computer games.

Dad had another surprise for them.

"You know when you went out with Mum and Sarah the other week," Dad reminded them. "Well I wasn't doing jobs like I told you, I was actually doing a bit of recording and here it is."

Dad proudly gave the children a CD which said 'Happy birthday Jimmy and Charlie' on the cover.

"A CD for us? Wow, Dad that's great!" said an excited Jimmy. "Let's put it on now!" And he rushed over to the CD player and music with Dad's voice singing started to fill the air. There was a song about me! Yes me! I couldn't believe it. It was so catchy that within seconds everyone had started to join in with the chorus. There were three more songs. One about me and my friends, one about Jimmy and Charlie and the last one was a happy birthday song.

"Oh Dad," said Charlie with tears in her eyes giving Dad a big hug, "that's the best birthday present ever, you're so clever!"

"It was easy," replied Dad modestly. "I only wrote songs about all the things that have happened to us, it was great fun to do."

"Could we do a version with me and Charlie joining in?" suggested Jimmy. What a great idea, I thought. I hoped I could join in as well, so I started to bark and jump around.

"Of course we can," said Dad, "and don't worry, we won't forget you Chico, you can join in as well."

Great, I couldn't wait!

"In fact Jimmy you could help me, I could show you how to use the computer to record."

"Wow!" said Jimmy. "That would be fantastic, I might even try writing a song myself."

Dad had a big grin on his face, Jimmy was jumping around shouting 'Yippee', Charlie was grinning and humming the Chico song and Mum was quietly smiling.

This is how it should be, I thought to myself.

After breakfast they rushed outside with balloons and streamers and with Dad's help decorated the boat. Whichwey looked lovely. People were having coffee at a little café, on the quayside next to the boat. They came over to admire Whichwey and asked the children what the occasion was. The children excitedly told them how it was their seventh birthday and that they were having a party.

At one o'clock Gran arrived with Harold, the handyman from Gran's home. She told us how he had kindly offered to bring her in his car.

"Oh, it was no bother really," Harold told us. "Dotty told me about your narrowboat and I was curious to come and have a look anyway."

"Well, you're very welcome but it's still very kind of you, Harold," replied Mum.

Mum showed them both down into the boat and gave them a cup of tea. Harold kept saying how lovely the boat was and how lucky we were to be living aboard.

Gran just made sniffing noises and I could hear her muttering under her breath. I thought I just caught the sound of the word 'Ridiculous!'

"Now Gran we need you to do us a big favour," said Charlie in a serious voice.

"Depends what it is," said Gran looking suspicious.

"You know how marvellous you were when you saved, Chico?"

Gran suddenly looked very pleased with herself.

"Harold!" she bellowed.

"Yes Dotty?"

"Did I tell you," she continued, still shouting. "How I saved the dog?" Harold was standing right behind her,

"Yes you did Dotty, you noticed he had fallen into the canal and you alerted everyone so he could be pulled to safety," replied Harold.

"Exactly!" said Gran smugly.

Harold winked at Charlie and me and whispered, "She's told everyone, at least a dozen times!"

Charlie giggled and continued. "Well, Gran, we need someone to look after Chico for us when we are busy with the party. He seems to be getting into more mischief lately and we don't want him to get into trouble today."

'Trouble!' What a cheek! I didn't get into trouble! It was trouble that seemed to get into me!

Gran was looking at me now with a funny kind of grin on her face. Was she remembering the first time we met and how I tripped her up? Was it going to be revenge today?

"Of course," she replied in a sickly sort of voice. "Harold and I would love to look after Chico. Now come here Chico."

It was the first time she had called me by my name instead of 'Dog' and it felt rather strange. She bent down to stroke me, but I started to back away slowly with my tail between my legs.

"We're best of friends these days aren't we, Chico?"

I wasn't so sure!

It was two o' clock and Emily was the first to arrive.

Charlie looked so pleased to see her and she had tears in her eyes as they squealed, hugged and danced around flapping their arms madly. Charlie showed her around Whichwey.

"Oh, it's lovely," cooed Emily. "You're *so* lucky, Charlotte!"

"Call me Charlie from now on," said Charlie, looking very pleased with herself.

Then Marc and his mum arrived. Jimmy was so excited to see them again and showed them around the boat talking about all the adventures they'd had over the last few weeks. All their friends kept saying how lucky they were and what fun it must be living on a boat.

George and Beth came with their mum and dad. The twins were really pleased to see them and Flossy looked far more relaxed this time.

"You look great!" I told her.

"Well things are much better at home now. Since our holiday on the canal Mum and Dad decided they were going to spend more time with Beth, George and me. Most weekends we go for walks to the park, we play together and everyone seems a lot happier."

The children were able to play the games that the twins had organised on the quayside. There was plenty of room as we were the only boat moored. The sun was shining and the sky was blue, everyone was having a lovely time. Mum brought the food outside and everyone laughed and chatted as they tucked into pizzas, crisps and sandwiches.

I was having fun talking to Flossy and telling her about chasing ducks with Scrappy.

"Trust you Chico!" She smiled. "Life always seems to be fun when you're around."

I smiled to myself and looked around for Gran.

Thank goodness, she seemed to have forgotten about me and was in deep conversation with Harold.

While Flossy and I were catching up Mum came out with the birthday cake on a large plate and took it over to the twins who were standing next to the back of the boat. This was the bit I had been looking forward to. I had seen the cake and it was divided into two halves. One side was for Charlie and was purple with delicate icing flowers and the other was green with tiny little plastic footballers looking as if they were running around. There were fourteen candles on it, because Jimmy had seven on his side of the cake and Charlie had seven on hers.

Suddenly all the children were crowding around singing Happy Birthday. Oh no, they'd started without me! I couldn't see! I needed to get a better look!

I looked over to check that Gran wasn't watching me. Where was she? Harold was standing quite close to the twins, but I couldn't see Gran anywhere. Quickly I managed to squeeze my way in between everyone's legs just in time to be standing next to Jimmy and Charlie as they blew out the candles.

Oh no! I'd missed it! I started to bark and jump up and down, I still couldn't see properly. Suddenly I was being lifted into the air. It was Dad, he must have noticed me and he'd lifted me up to see!

"Don't forget Chico!" he shouted. "He wants to join in as well."

"And don't forget me!" came a shrill voice from, yes you've guessed it... Gran!

She was elbowing her way through the crowd of children, waving her stick in the air.

"Oh dear," sighed Dad.

"Come on then Dotty, that's right everyone… move out the way… let Gran through."

This was when I noticed that the candles on the cake, even though they'd been blown out had relit themselves and were burning brightly again. Oh… they were *magic* candles!

"Let me have the camera," Harold said taking it from Dad.

"You've got your hands full with Chico. Get ready for a photo then!" he called, pointing the camera at the cake.

"Come on Chico," said Jimmy, "you help us this time. Ready? All blow together after three…"

Now I don't know if you know this but dogs can't blow. I did try really hard though and as the children all started to count I got my nose closer and closer to the candles.

This is when it all became a bit of a blur…

"One…!" Suddenly my nose began to tickle…

"Two…!" Oh no… was I going to…? Yes… I think I was…

"Ahhhh… tchoooo!"

As the children reached 'three' I sneezed an almighty sneeze all over the cake and one of the little plastic footballers from Jimmy's half flew off and hit Gran right on the nose! She yelped and fell backwards in surprise. As she fell her leg stuck out in front of her and she kicked the bottom of the plate the cake was on. There was complete silence as the cake and the plate flew past everyone in what felt like slow motion until, with a loud splash, they landed together in the canal. In the silence that followed all I could hear was the clicking of the camera.

"CHICO!" shouted the twins at the same time.

Oh no! Now that wasn't fair... it wasn't me that kicked the cake in the water but I had the feeling I was in trouble again. Dad had put me down and as I looked up everyone was staring at me, even Flossy. Gran was rubbing the end of her nose and giving me a very scary stare. I was beginning to wish I hadn't bothered to help with blowing out the candles at all! Beth and George looked at Jimmy and Charlie and they all looked at me.

"Trust you Chico!" giggled Charlie. Well you know how contagious giggling is, before long Jimmy and Marc were giggling, then Beth and George. Another child started to giggle and then another and another and before long everyone including Mum and Dad was laughing. Everyone except Gran... she still looked very cross!

Mum managed to calm Gran down before Harold took her home. Harold said he hadn't had so much fun in ages and hoped the photos would turn out well.

Later that night when Dad had gone off to his gig and the children had helped Mum tidy up, Jimmy got out the laptop to look at the photos.

There were some lovely pictures of Jimmy and Charlie and all their friends, but the best ones were the action shots Harold had taken. There were 4 pictures in sequence. The first showed Gran with a horrified look on her face. She was in the process of falling backwards and I looked as if I was in the middle of an enormous sneeze.

The second was the cake and plate in mid air with shocked expressions on everyone's faces.

The third was of a large splash in the water with the cake disappearing and the last one was of a couple of magic candles floating on the surface.

Who would have believed a year ago that the twins' seventh birthday would be on a boat? I certainly wouldn't have! Mum and Dad seemed much happier these days and Jimmy and Charlie had never got on so well, Okay, they still had their moments, but generally they seemed a lot happier. We definitely felt like a family again and I couldn't be more content. I loved having company and had found our new life very exciting so far. Later that night as I was lying in my basket I could hear Jimmy and Charlie talking in bed.

"You know what?" Charlie whispered to Jimmy.

"I know I always said I wouldn't like living on a boat, but I've changed my mind. I love it! That was the best birthday ever!"

"Yes it was," mumbled a very sleepy Jimmy.

"Even if we never got to eat the cake... I don't think anyone will forget our seventh birthday!"

Well, I knew I wouldn't.

END